How do I use this scheme?

Key Words with Peter and Jane has three
parallel series, each containing twelve books. All three
series are written using the same carefully controlled
vocabulary. Readers will get the most out of **Key Words** with
Peter and Jane when they follow the books in the pattern
1a, 1b, 1c; 2a, 2b, 2c and so on.

• Series a
gradually introduces and repeats new words.

• Series b
provides further practice of these same words, but
in a different context and with different illustrations.

• Series c
uses familiar words to teach **phonics** in a methodical way,
enabling children to read increasingly difficult words.
It also provides a link to writing.

Published by Ladybird Books Ltd
A Penguin Company
Penguin Books Ltd., 80 Strand, London WC2R 0RL, UK
Penguin Books Australia Ltd., Camberwell, Victoria, Australia
Penguin Group (NZ) 67 Apollo Drive, Rosedale, North Shore 0632, New Zealand

1 3 5 7 9 10 8 6 4 2

ISBN: 978-1-40930-149-3

Printed in China

Key Words

with Peter and Jane

2b

Have a go

written by W. Murray
illustrated by J.H. Wingfield

I like the dog.

You like the dog.

You and I like the dog

you   You

I like trees.

You like trees.

You and I like trees.

You want toys.

I want toys.

You and I want toys.

want

You like Peter.

I like Peter.

We like Peter.

we   We

I like Jane.

You like Jane.

We like Jane.

Jane

Here are shops.

We like shops.

We like toy shops.

are

You can fish.

I can fish.

We can fish.

can fish

You want fun.

I want fun.

This is fun.

fun   this   This

This is Pat.

I like Pat.

Pat likes fun.

We like this dog.

Pat

Here is some water.

some water

I like the water.

Here is Peter
and here is Jane.

Here you are,
Jane and Peter.

Here is some water.

Look in the water.

You are in the water

Here is Peter.

He likes water.

He has the dog.

The dog is
in the water.

He likes it.

he He it

Jane has a ball.

It is for Pat.

Pat is here.

He wants the ball.

for

Here is a tree.

Pat looks into the tree.

He looks for Peter
and Jane.

They are in the tree.

into they They

Look here, says Jane.

Look here, Peter.

Come and look.

Peter comes, and
they look.

says   comes   Come

Here are some sweets.

Some are for Peter
and some for Jane.

They have some sweets.

They like sweets.

sweets   have

Peter wants to jump
and Pat wants to jump

They jump for fun.

Can you jump this?
says Peter to Jane.

to jump

Yes, says Jane.
Yes, I can jump this.

I want to jump.

Look, Peter, look.

I can jump this.

yes   Yes

Peter and Jane
go to the shop.
They go into the shop
for some fish.

Peter has the dog,
and Jane has the fish.

go

41

The fish go into the water.

Into the water they go.

Pat wants the fish.

no No

No, Pat, no, says Peter.

No, no, no, says Jane
to the dog.

Peter and Jane have fun

Here comes Peter .

Here comes Jane .

Here they come .

We like this, they say .

Have a go,
says Jane to Peter.

Yes, says Peter.

He has a go.
You have a go,
says Peter to Jane.
Jane has a go.

Have some,
says Jane to Peter.

Yes, says Peter.

You have some, Jane
says Peter.

Yes, I like it, Jane says.

ICES

49

Here they go.

Jane wants to go home.
Peter wants to go home.
and the dog wants
to go home.

Yes, we want to go home,
they say.

home

New words used in this book

Page		Page	
4	you	26	he it
8	want	28	for
10	we	30	into they
14	are	32	says come
16	can fish	34	sweets have
18	fun this	36	to jump
20	Pat	38	yes
22	some water	40	go
24	look	42	no
		50	home

Total number of new words: 27
Average repetition per word: 9